MARK TWAIN, born Samuel Langhorne Clemens, spent his cherished years of boyhood in Hannibal, Mo., on the Mississippi River. Two of his most famous books, *Tom Sawyer* and *Huckleberry Finn,* depict many of his own experiences in this picturesque locale. He drifted into the literary world by becoming a printer's apprentice. In later years he was to become increasingly better known as a printer, river pilot, newspaper reporter, world traveler, lecturer and author. His principal writings are characterized by a simple style, rich in humor and philosophy, resulting in pure and unsurpassed Americana.

Mark Twain's

THE ADVENTURES OF
Huckleberry Finn

Abridged and Adapted by MARY CUSHING
Illustrated by CASEY JONES

GROSSET & DUNLAP · Publishers · NEW YORK

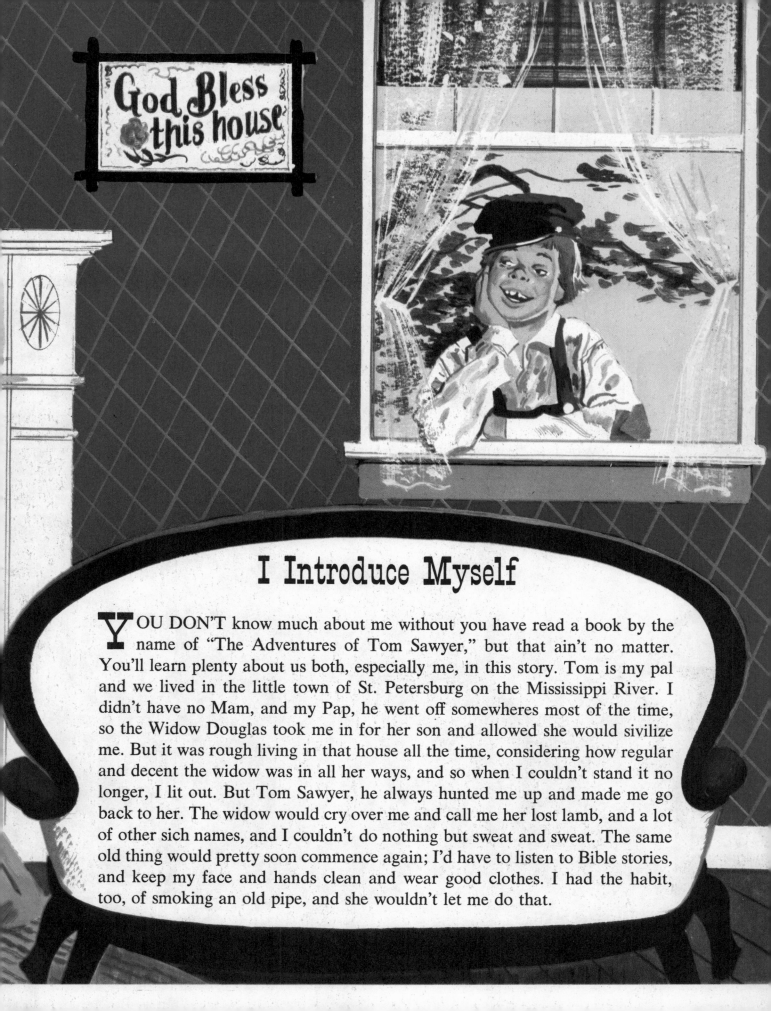

I Introduce Myself

YOU DON'T know much about me without you have read a book by the name of "The Adventures of Tom Sawyer," but that ain't no matter. You'll learn plenty about us both, especially me, in this story. Tom is my pal and we lived in the little town of St. Petersburg on the Mississippi River. I didn't have no Mam, and my Pap, he went off somewheres most of the time, so the Widow Douglas took me in for her son and allowed she would sivilize me. But it was rough living in that house all the time, considering how regular and decent the widow was in all her ways, and so when I couldn't stand it no longer, I lit out. But Tom Sawyer, he always hunted me up and made me go back to her. The widow would cry over me and call me her lost lamb, and a lot of other sich names, and I couldn't do nothing but sweat and sweat. The same old thing would pretty soon commence again; I'd have to listen to Bible stories, and keep my face and hands clean and wear good clothes. I had the habit, too, of smoking an old pipe, and she wouldn't let me do that.

Miss Watson, the widow's sister, lived with us. She was a tolerable slim old maid, and was always pecking at me. All I ever wanted was to go off somewheres for a change, but she said that if I wouldn't mind her, I'd never go to Heaven. Well, if *she* was going to be there, it would be no place for me. So I set one night in my room, thinking instead of sleeping, and pretty soon I hear a twig snap in the dark outside. I could just barely make out a little *"meow, meow,"* so I answered as soft as I could, put out the light, and scrambled out the window, over the lean-to and down to the ground. There among the trees was Tom Sawyer a-waiting for me.

We went right off tiptoeing along the garden path, and as we was passing by the kitchen I happened to see Miss Watson's big Negro, Jim, setting there in the doorway. We liked Jim, but we also liked to play tricks on him, so Tom took Jim's hat and hung it right on a tree-limb over his head, and we knowed that when Jim woke up he'd be sure to think them old witches was after him.

When we got back in my room, we talked a long time, and decided to plan some real good adventures as soon as ever we could.

Well, I got a good "going over" in the morning from old Miss Watson on account of the way my clothes looked from sliding down the roof, and she took me in a closet and prayed, but nothing come of it. It didn't prevent me for a minute going right on adventuring with Tom.

We played robbers now and then for about a month, but we didn't rob nobody, didn't kill any people, only just pretended, but that was what Tom liked and sometimes I think he believed all the things that he made up himself.

Three or four months run along and it was well into the winter now. I had been to school most all this time and could spell and read and write quite a bit, and could say the multiplication table up to six times seven is thirty-five. At first I hated school, but by and by I got so I could stand it. Whenever I was kinda tired of it, I played hooky, and the thrashing I got for it next day done me good and cheered me up. But living in a house and sleeping in a bed pulled on me pretty tight, and before the cold weather come I used to slide out sometimes and just sleep in the woods.

One night when I went up to my room to bed and was lighting my candle I looked around sudden and there sat my Pap — his own self — who I hadn't laid an eye on for a mighty long while. I was always kinda scared of Pap, 'cause he used to whip me good whenever he got mad. He looked pretty poorly; his face had no color in it at all, his hair was all long, tangled and greasy, and his clothes were in awful rags. He was down on his luck and wanted me to go away with him and look after him. I sure didn't want to; I said I had to go to school. So then he says he'd cowhide me till I was black and blue if I didn't raise some money for him somehow. He was always after me to get him money, and I'd borrow a few dollars for him if I could, and Pap would take it and get drunk and make such a disturbance that he'd land in jail every time.

Well, just to spite him, I wouldn't give up school, and he got to hanging around the widow's house too much and she told him that if he didn't quit loafing around there she'd make trouble for him. Well, wasn't he mad! He said he'd show her who was Huck Finn's boss, so he watched out for me one day and catched me, and took me up the river about three miles in a skiff and crossed over to the Illinois shore where it was woody and there warn't no houses, just an old log hut in a place where the timber was thick.

We lived in that ole cabin and he always locked the door and put the key under his head nights. He had a gun, too, which he had stole, and we fished and hunted and that was what we lived on, and once in awhile he'd go to the store to trade game for grocery stuff, but he always locked me in when he went off. Much as I craved to get free, I found I was kind of liking the life just the same. It was lazy and jolly, laying off comfortable all day, smoking and fishing, and no books nor study.

Two months or more run along like that, and by and by Pap got too handy with his hick'ry and I just couldn't stand it. He got to go away too much, locking me up like a prisoner, and I was getting scared. I made up my mind I'd got to fix up some way to get out of there. So I started looking around and finally I found what I wanted. It was an old wood-saw laid up on a rafter. I greased it the best I could and went to work on a big bottom log, behind a horse-blanket that was put up to keep the wind from blowing through the chinks. It was a good long job, having to stop whenever Pap come back, and hide the saw. The night he was the drunkest he dozed right off after he come in, and I got a good chance to steal his gun, but he roused sudden and says, "What you doin' with my gun?"

So I says, "Somebody tried to get in, so I was a-laying for him, but he come no further."

"Well, all right then, go out and see if there's a fish on the line for breakfast."

He unlocked the door pretty careless like and I cleared out up the river bank.

I noticed there was some pieces of limbs and such things floating down, so I knowed the river had begun to rise. I went on along the bank, with one eye out for Pap and t'other one out for what the rise might fetch along. Well, all at once here comes a canoe — just a beauty, too, about fourteen foot long, but not a soul in it. It was sure enough a drift canoe, so I swum right out and clumb in it and paddled it ashore. I judged I'd better hide it good, and then when the time come to run off, it would be there for me to use. As soon as I'd done it, I went back to the cabin and we had our catfish for breakfast, and then we laid off for the day.

When evening come, the river was sure rising fast, and Pap decided he'd go out and see what he could salvage, so he locked me in and took the skiff and started off towing the raft. I judged he'd never come back that night. I waited till I reckoned he'd got a good start, then I out with my saw and went to work on that log again. Before he was t'other side of the river, I was out of the hole and him and his raft was just a speck on the water.

Now I had to load up the canoe with provisions for my get-away. I took a sack of corn meal that Pap had stole and dragged it over and put it in the canoe, then a side of bacon, some coffee, sugar, and all of the ammunition. I took fish line and matches, and I wanted an axe, but there wasn't any, only the one by the woodpile, and I knowed why I was going to leave that behind.

I fetched out the gun and now I was done, and only had to put the log back in place. It was all grass clear to the canoe, so I hadn't left any track, and nobody was on the river, so all was safe. I took the gun then and went hunting birds up in the woods when I suddenly see a wild pig. I shot this fellow right there and took him back to the camp. Then I took the axe and smashed in the door, and hacked open the pig's throat and laid him out on the ground to bleed. Next I took an old sack and put a lot of big rocks and the pig's body in it, and pulled it along through the door into the woods down to the river and dumped it in. It sunk straight down. You could easy see that something heavy and bleeding had been dragged along the ground.

I sure did wish Tom Sawyer was there. I knowed he would take an interest in this kind of business and throw in some fancy touches besides.

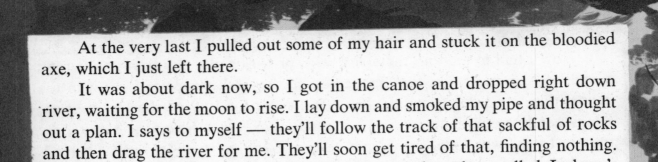

At the very last I pulled out some of my hair and stuck it on the bloodied axe, which I just left there.

It was about dark now, so I got in the canoe and dropped right down river, waiting for the moon to rise. I lay down and smoked my pipe and thought out a plan. I says to myself — they'll follow the track of that sackful of rocks and then drag the river for me. They'll soon get tired of that, finding nothing. All right, so I can stop anywhere I want to and that place called Jackson's Island is good enough for me.

I know that island pretty well and nobody never comes there. I can paddle over to town nights and slink around and pick up things I want. I didn't lose no time. The next minute I was spinning downstream soft but quick. When I got well below the ferry landing, where people might have seen me, I straightened up and see the island right there not far away, big and dark, and solid, like a steamboat without any lights. I got over there in no time and ran the canoe into a deep bend in the bank that I knowed about, behind some willow branches, and when I'd made fast nobody would of ever seen the canoe from the outside. There was a little gray in the sky now, so I stepped into the woods, and laid down for a nap before breakfast.

I Find Jim

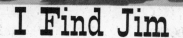

W HEN I WOKE up, the sun was up high and I was powerful lazy and comfortable. I guess I was dozing off again when I hears a deep sound of "Boom!" away up the river. I hopped up and peeked out of a hole in the leaves and see a bunch of smoke laying on the water a long ways up. I knowed what was the matter now. *Boom!* I see the white smoke squirt out of the ferryboat's side. You see, they was firing cannon over the water, trying to make my carcass come to the top.

I lit my pipe and went on watching. The ferryboat was floating with the current and I allowed I'd have a chance to see who was aboard when she come along. By and by she drifted in so close that they could of run out a plank and walked ashore. Most everybody I know was on the boat, talking about the murder, I could hear 'em plain. Then the captain broke in and says, "Stand away! Maybe he's washed ashore and got tangled among the brush at the water's edge."

Just then the cannon let off such a blast right before me that it made me deef with the noise and pretty near blind with smoke, and I judged I was a goner. But soon I see I warn't hurt, thanks to goodness! The boat floated on and went out of sight around the shoulder of the island, and I couldn't hear no more booming, so I knowed I was all right now. Nobody else would come a-hunting after me.

I got my traps out of the canoe and made me a nice camp in the thick woods. After that I set out my lines, lit a good fire and settled in. And so for three days and nights, no difference, just the same thing. The fourth day I went exploring around down through the island, and while I went fooling through the deep woods, I suddenly bounded right onto the ashes of a campfire that was still smoking. My heart jumped up, so then I clumb a tree to spy around a little. Pretty soon when nobody come, I got down, but I kept worrying that someone might be following me, and said to myself, I just can't live this way. I got to find out who it is that's here on the island with me.

So I take my paddle and slips out from shore and then let the canoe drop along down amongst the shadows. I poked along about an hour and was most down to the foot of the island, and sure enough, there I catched a glimpse of a fire away through the trees. I went for it cautious and slow until I was close enough to get a good look, and there laid a man on the ground. I set there behind a clump of bushes and kept my eyes on him steady. Pretty soon he yawned and stretched himself, and *it was Miss Watson's Jim!* I bet I was glad to see him!

I says, "Hello, Jim," and skipped out. He bounced up and stared at me wild. Then he kneels down and puts his hands together and moans:

"Doan' hurt me! I hain't ever done no harm to a ghos'. I alwuz liked dead peoples en done all I could for 'em. You go en git in the river agin, whar you b'longs en doan' do nuffin to Ole Jim."

Well, I warn't long making him understand I warn't dead. Now I knew I wouldn't be lonesome no more. But he only set there and looked at me and never said nothing.

When we settled around the fire, I asked him how long he'd been here.

"I come to the island de night arter you's killed."

"Ain't you most starved?"

"Sure 'nuf, I reckon I could eat a horse."

So we went to the canoe, got some provisions, made a fire and had a fine breakfast, then sat around talking and Jim asked me, "Say, Huck, who wuz it dat 'uz killed in dat shanty if it warn't you?"

So I told him the whole thing and he said it was right smart, and that even Tom Sawyer couldn't get up a better plan.

Then I says, "And how did *you* come to be here?"

He looks pretty uneasy at that and says perhaps he'd better not tell, but I kept at him and promised not to tell on him if he'd trust me with the whole story. So he did.

"I . . . I run away from Miss Watson. One night I overheered her fixin' to sell me to a slave-trader from Orleans for eight hundred dollars, en it 'uz sich a big stack uv money I knowed she couldn't resis'. I never waited to hear the res'. I lit out mighty quick, I tell you. It was already pooty dark, so I took up along de river road. A raff 'uz what I 'uz after, so when I see one a-comin' roun' de pint, I swum out to de stern of it quiet-like and took a-holt. But when I see dere wuz folks aboard, I slid off again and struck for de island, and here I is."

Now, in about the middle of the island there was a great big rock with a cave in it that I knowed about, and I reckoned we could hide real comfortable there. So we went and hauled up all our provisions and stuff to it, and settled down. It was better'n home. That night while we was eating our supper, I says, "Jim, this is sure nice. I wouldn't want to be anywhere else but right here. Pass me along another hunk of fish and some o' that hot corn pone!"

One night when we was up at the head of the island, here comes a frame house a-floating right by us. We paddled out and clumb aboard and in at an upstairs window. We could make out a bed, a table, and two chairs, and there was something laying on the floor in the far corner that looked like a man.

Jim called out, "Hello, you!"

But the thing didn't budge, and after we both hollered again, Jim says, "Dat man ain't asleep — he's dead! If you comes in, Huck, don't you look at him, it's too gashly!"

So Jim threw some old rags over the corpse and let it lay. While we was there we thought we'd better look around to see if there was something we could use. We found some dirty old calico dresses, a sunbonnet, and some men's clothing too, none of it much good, but we took them. There was all kinds of house stuff too, like candles, a lantern and some knives, and so, take it all around, we made a pretty good haul, especially when we was rummaging through the clothes and found all of eight dollars sewed up in the lining of an old overcoat. That was luck. We pushed off in the canoe with Jim laying down under a quilt so no one could see him, and we got home all safe and sound.

The days passed along and the river went down between its banks again, and as things were getting a little slow and dull, I thought I oughter get a stirring-up some way, so I reckoned I'd slip over to the mainland and find out what was going on. Jim said I ought to go in the dark and look out pretty sharp, so we decided I would dress up as a girl. We shortened one of the calico gowns and I turned up my trouser legs to my knees and got into it, and it was a fair fit. I put on the sunbonnet and tied it under my chin and Jim said nobody would know me hardly.

One night I met up with a friendly old woman who said, "You hadn't ought to be out alone, honey. There's been a murder around here lately." So then she went right on and told me all about Pap and how he probably killed me. Everybody thought that at first, but later on they changed and judged it was done by a runaway slave named Jim.

"That Negro ran off the very same night Huck Finn was killed, and there's a reward out for him of three hundred dollars!"

"Does everybody think that Negro done it?"

"No, not all, but they'll get that feller pretty soon now and maybe they can scare the truth out of him."

"They still chasin' him, then?"

"Yes, some folks think he ain't far from here, because I'm pretty sure I seen smoke over on Jackson's Island a couple of days ago. My husband and another man are fixin' to go over there right after midnight and see what it is."

I didn't stop even to thank her, I just left. I had to warn Jim. On the way across the water I hear the clock strike eleven, so I hurried fast to the camp. Soon as I landed, I ran into the cave and waked Jim up.

"Hump yourself, Jim, there ain't a minute to lose! They're after us!"

We grabbed everything we had and stowed it on the raft, hitched up the canoe and started off down the river. But we was floating so slow we was afraid to be seen, so when the first streak of day begun to show, we tied up to a towhead, where we hacked off branches and covered up the raft, and Jim took some of the top planks off and built us a snug little wigwam to shelter us.

Fallen Grandeur

I T WAS kind of solemn drifting down that big, still river, laying on our backs and looking up at the stars. We had mighty good weather for quite a spell and nothing really happened to us. Every night we passed towns, some of them way up on black hillsides, nothing but just a shiny bed of lights — not a house could you see. The fifth night we passed the city of St. Louis and it was like the whole world lit up. We drifted on along the river doing pretty well for ourselves, slipping ashore now and again to buy a few things and sometimes I even stole a watermelon for us.

Two, three nights swum by. It was a monstrous big river down there, sometimes a mile and a half wide. We run nights and hid up daytimes as usual, taking it easy, swimming, fishing, and eating. It's lovely to live on a raft, but it does get lonesome when there is no sign of other folks on the water.

So again I went ashore one day looking to pick some berries for us. Just as I was passing a place where a cow-path crossed a crick, here comes a couple of men tearing up the path as tight as they could foot it. I tried to give them the slip, but they was too close to me and sung out and begged *me* to save their lives, saying that they hadn't been doing nothing but was being chased for it by men with dogs. I couldn't just exactly believe them, but I agreed to take them on aways. They got into the canoe with me and we lit out for the towhead where Jim and the raft was hid.

One of these fellows had a bald head and very gray whiskers and was dressed like a tramp, and the other fellow was some younger and dressed about as ornery. They was both carrying carpet bags. We fed 'em some breakfast on the raft and while we was talking it come out that these chaps didn't even know one another, but they had one point in common — each one was in a pack of trouble. It seems that they had been deceiving folks with all kinds of tricks, selling worthless stuff and telling lies. Each one allowed that if he hadn't beat it quick out of town, he'd of been tarred and feathered.

"Old man," said the young one, "why don't we double-team it together? What do you think?"

"I ain't undisposed. What's your line — mainly?"

The young one tells how he's been a printer by trade, done a little in patent medicines, some theater acting, teached singing, geography, slinging a lecture sometimes . . . in fact, most anything that came handy, just so it warn't work.

So then the old one says, "I've done considerable in the doctorin' way, layin' on o' hands, and sich. I can tell a fortune pretty good, preachin' is another of my lines, and workin' camp meetin's and missionaryin' around."

Then the young fellow hove a big sigh, and says, "Alas, to think I should have lived to be leading such a life and be degraded down into such company! I've brought myself down pretty far!"

"Brought yourself down from whar?" asks the old man.

"Ah, you wouldn't believe me, but let it pass! Well, if you must know, the secret of my birth is that, gentlemen, by rights I am a duke."

All of our eyes bugged out when we heard that. Then the bald-head says, "No! You can't mean it!"

"Yes, sir. My great-grandfather, eldest son of the Duke of Bridgewater, fled to this country about the end of last century, married here and died, leaving a son. I am the lineal descendant of that son, and here am I, forlorn, torn from my high estate, hunted of men, despised by a cold world, ragged, worn, heartbroken, and degraded to the companionship of felons on rafts!"

We tried to comfort him, and he told us that the best way would be to acknowledge him by bowing to him when we spoke to him and saying, "Your Grace" or "My Lord" or "Your Lordship." Then he says, too, he wouldn't mind really if we just called him plain Bridgewater, but one of us ought to wait on him at dinner. By this time the older man got pretty silent — he seemed to have something heavy on his mind.

"Lookee here, Bilgewater," he says, "I'm mighty sorry for you, but you ain't the only person that's had troubles, nor had a secret of your birth."

And by jinks, he began to cry real tears.

"Kin I trust you?" he says.

"To the bitter death!" says the Duke. And he took the old man's hand and squeezed it. "Speak!"

"Bilgewater, I am the late Dauphin. Your eyes is looking at this very moment at the pore, disappeared Dauphin, Looy the Seventeen, son of Looy the Sixteen and Marry Antonette."

"You! At your age? No! You mean you're the late Charlemagne. You must be six or seven hundred years old at the very least."

"Trouble has done it, Bilgewater. Trouble has brung these gray hairs and this premature balditude. Yes, gentlemen, you see before you in blue jeans and misery the wanderin', exiled, trampled-on and sufferin' rightful King of France!"

Well, he cried and took on so that me and Jim didn't know hardly what to do, we was so sorry, but glad and proud, too, so we waited on him first at meals and always called him "Your Majesty."

This done him heaps of good, so he got cheerful and comfortable, but the Duke kind of soured on it, and stayed huffy a good while till the King says, "Cheer up, it ain't your fault you was only born a duke and I a king. Likely we'll be together on this raft a blame long time, so why worry?"

Well, it sure didn't take me long to make up my mind that these liars warn't no kings nor dukes at all, but just low-down humbugs and frauds, but I never said nothing.

They asked us considerable many questions, wanted to know what we covered up the raft that way for and laid by in the daytime instead of traveling. Was Jim a runaway slave?

Says I, "Goodness sakes, would a runaway slave run *south?*"

No, they allowed he wouldn't.

But as I did have to account for Jim somehow or other, we let on that he belonged to me. I said to them, "You ain't the first ones that thinks he's a runaway. People is always coming out in boats to ask, for they're after the rewards, so we don't run daytimes no more now. Nights no one bothers us."

The Duke said he was a-going to figure out a way so we could travel in daylight too, if we wanted to. By and by he says to the King, "Have you ever been on the stage, Royalty?"

The King said he hadn't and then the Duke tells him, "You shall, then, before you are three days older, Fallen Grandeur. The first good town we come to, we'll hire a hall and do the sword-fight in Richard III and the balcony scene in Romeo and Juliet. How does that strike you?"

"I'm in up to the hub for anything that will pay, Bilgewater, but I don't know nothin' about play-actin' and hain't ever seen much of it. I was too small when Pap used to have them at the Palace. Do you reckon you could learn me?"

"Easy!"

The Duke said that he was used to being Romeo, so the King could play Juliet, and give the book to him so he could get his part by heart. He wouldn't have to worry about costumes, for we had enough of 'em, and a good actor ought to be able to play anything.

Praying and Playing

NOW THERE was a little one-horse town about three mile down the bend, and so we all went ashore where they was having, of all things, a camp meeting. The King was mighty pleased at this circumstance and got directions right away so he could go and work it for all it was worth, and he let me go along, too. The Duke just naturally went looking for a printing office, and there we left him to prowl.

When we got to the meeting place, there was as much as a thousand people there. The preaching was going on under sheds and the first one we come to, the preacher was lining out a hymn. Everybody sung it and it was grand to hear. Then the preacher begun to preach with all the people shouting, "Glory! A-a-men! Oh, come to the mourners' bench! Come, black with sin."

First thing I knowed the King got a-going and you could hear him over everybody. So the preacher begged him to speak to the people and he willingly done it. He told them he'd been a pirate for thirty years out in the Indian Ocean and his crew was thinned out considerable last spring in a fight. So he was home now to take out some fresh men, even though he'd been robbed just the night before, which he said was the blessedest thing that ever happened to him because he was a changed man now. He was going to start right off and work his way back to the Indian Ocean and put in the rest of his life trying to turn the pirates into the true path. Then he busted into tears and so did everybody. And, like he hoped they would, somebody sings out, "Take up a collection for him! Let him pass the hat around."

So the King did just that, going through the crowd with his hat, swabbing his eyes, and blessing the people and praising them, and thanking them for being so good to the pore pirates away off there!

When we got back to the raft and he come to count up his takings, he found it was eighty-seven dollars and seventy-five cents. The Duke said he'd been doing pretty well, too, all this time. He'd done a little printing job with a picture of a runaway Negro on it, and there was *"$200 Reward"* writ under it. The reading was all about Jim and just described him to the dot.

So the Duke explained to us, "Now we can run in the daytime if we want to. Whenever we see anybody coming, we can tie Jim hand and foot and lay him in the wigwam and show this handbill and say we captured him up the river and were too poor to travel on a steamboat and are on our way down to get the reward." At this we all agreed the Duke was pretty smart.

They were awake and studying their parts, however, around sunup next morning, and the first chance we got, the Duke had some showbills printed and after that, for two or three days as we floated along, the raft was a most uncommon lively place, with nothing but sword-fighting and rehearsing.

One morning, when we was pretty well down the state of Arkansaw, we come in sight of a shabby little town in a big bend of the river and found out that there was going to be a circus there that afternoon. So the two "actors" decided that as the circus would be leaving before night, our show would have a pretty good chance with all those people there.

So the Duke, he hired the courthouse and we went around and stuck up our bills. Then we went loafing round town until evening, when we had our show, but there warn't only about twelve people there, just enough to pay expenses. They laughed all the time and that made the Duke mad, and everybody left, anyway, before the show was over. The Duke complained that these Arkansaw lunkheads couldn't come up to Shakespeare, what they wanted was low comedy. So next morning he got some big sheets of wrapping paper and some black paint, and drawed off some new handbills and stuck them all over the village. The bills said:

For Three Nights Only!
Come See the King's Camel-leopard!
Or the Royal Nonesuch!
LADIES AND CHILDREN NOT ADMITTED!

"There," says he, "if that last line don't fetch 'em, I don't know Arkansaw."

Well, all day him and the King was hard at it, rigging up a stage and a curtain and a row of candles for footlights, and that night the house was jammed full of men in no time. When the place couldn't hold no more, the Duke stood before the curtain and made a little speech, and said this was the most thrillingest tragedy that ever was. At last, when he'd got everybody's expectations up high, he rolled up the curtain and the next minute the King come a-prancing out on all fours, naked, and he was painted all over, ring-streaked-and-striped all sorts of colors, as splendid as a rainbow. It was just wild, but it was awful funny. The people most killed themselves laughing and the King done it over and over again, and when the Duke finally lets down the curtain, the men all sings out, "What, is it over? Is that all?"

The Duke says, "Yes, but there will be more tomorrow."

Next day you couldn't hear nothing around that town but how splendid the show was, and the house was jammed again that night and again the next. I was standing in the door the third night, watching the folks coming in. Every last one of them had his pockets bulging and I see this warn't no parfumerie neither. I smelt sickly eggs, rotten cabbages, and such things, and even several dead cats.

When the hall was full up, the Duke pulled me behind the stage door and says, "Walk fast now till you get away from the houses, and then shin for the raft, like the dickens was after you."

We struck the raft about the same time and I reckoned the poor King was in for a gaudy time of it with the audience, but not at all. Pretty soon he crawls out from under the wigwam and says:

"Well, how'd the old thing pan out this time, Duke?"

He hadn't been up town at all, and the two of them fairly laughed their bones loose over the way they had served them people. In all, them two rapscallions took in four hundred and sixty-five dollars in those three nights.

Humbugs and Frauds

THE NEXT day the King begins to lay out another plan for working them hick towns. Jim complained a little now about being left alone all the time 'cause, you see, when nobody was there, we had to tie him, for if anybody should happen on to him there all by himself and not tied, it wouldn't look much like he was a runaway slave. The Duke was uncommon bright and he soon struck an idea. He dressed Jim up in one of our long curtain-calico gowns and a white horsehair wig and whiskers that he had among his theater stuff. Then he took some grease paint and colored Jim's face, hands, ears, and neck all over a dead dull solid blue, like a man that's been drownded. Then the Duke took and wrote out on a shingle, SICK ARAB — BUT HARMLESS WHEN NOT OUT OF HIS HEAD, and nailed it to a lathe and stood it up in front of the wigwam. Then Jim was satisfied 'cause he didn't have to be tied. But the Duke told him that if anybody come around, he must hop out and howl like a wild beast, so they would light out and leave him be.

Even though there was a powerful lot of money in it, the Duke and the King decided not to try the "Nonesuch" again so soon, for fear news of it might have traveled down the river, and something else had to be planned. The King allowed he'd drop over to the next village and just trust in Providence to lead him on the profitable way. Now the King and me was all dressed up in store clothes he'd bought, so we looked real respectable.

We jumps in the canoe and makes off. Pretty soon we come to a nice innocent-looking country jake setting on the bank.

"Run her nose inshore," says the King, and I done it. "Where you bound for, young man?"

"For the steamboat going to Orleens."

"Well, get aboard. My servant will help you with the bags." (Meaning me, I see.)

So the feller asks the King where he was going and the King told him he was going up a few mile to see an old friend on a farm.

"You know, when I first saw you," says the young man, "I thought you was Mr. Wilks. You ain't him, are you?"

"No, my name's Rev. Elexander Blodgett. But I'm jest as able to be sorry for Mr. Wilks for not arrivin' in time, if he's missed anything by it, which I hope he hasn't."

"Well, he missed seeing his brother Peter die, who would have given anything in the world to say good-by to him. Hadn't seen him since they was boys together and hadn't ever seen his brother William at all — that's the deef and dumb one. Except for the nieces who lived with him, Harvey and William's the only ones left now; and as I was saying, they haven't got here in time. He left a letter behind for Harvey, and he told in it where his money was hid and how he wanted the rest of the property divided up so the g'yirls would be all right."

At the mention of money, the King sure pricked up his ears, and went along questioning this young fellow all about the Wilks family, and their friends too. It appeared that Harvey and the deef-and-dumb brother was coming from England and that's why they was late. There was three girls, Mary Jane, Susan, and Joanna. Then the King went on asking, kind of anxious now, was Peter Wilks well off.

"Oh, yes, he had three-four thousand in cash hid up somewheres and some land and houses."

"When did you say he died?"

"I didn't say, but it was last night, and the funeral is set for tomorrow about midday."

So we took him on to the landing and left him.

I looked at the King kind of sharp and could see that now something new was in the wind. He told me to go back and fetch the Duke and hustle him up. So when I got back with the Duke, the King told him everything like the young fellow had said, and all the time he was telling it he was talking like an Englishman, and for a slouch he done it pretty good too.

Presently he says, "How are you on the deef-and-dumb, Bilgewater?"

The Duke says that with his experience in the theater he thought he could play most anything required. So we waited there for a slow boat to take us to the village and when we came ashore, there was a bunch of men waiting on the dock and the King says to them, "Kin any of you gentlemen tell me where Mr. Peter Wilks lives?"

They give a glance at one another. Then one of them answered soft and gentle, "I'm sorry, sir, but we can only tell you where he did live 'til last night."

Sudden as winking, the ornery old cretur went all to smash and put his chin on the man's shoulder and cried down his back, sobbing, "Alas, alas, our poor brother — gone, and we never got to see him! Oh, it's too, too hard!"

Then he turns around, blubbering, and makes a lot of idiotic signs with his hands to the Duke, and blamed if *he* didn't start a-crying. If they weren't the beatenest lot, them two frauds, that ever I struck. It was enough to make a body ashamed of the human race.

The news was all over town in two minutes with everybody saying, "Is it *them?*"

When we reached the house, the street in front of it was packed and the three girls was standing in the doorway. They was so overjoyed to see their "uncles" that they just jumped into their arms and kissed them. We went right in and there was the coffin standing on two chairs over in the corner. So then the King and the Duke, with a hand across each other's shoulders and t'other hand to their eyes, walked slow and solemn over to it. All the men took off their hats and dropped their heads. And when these "uncles" bent over and looked at the corpse, they bust out a-crying for nearly four minutes. I never saw two men cry the way they done.

By and by the King looks up and slobbers out a speech all full of tears and flapdoodle, and invites the intimate friends in the crowd to stay to supper with

him and his "nieces" and help set up the ashes of the deceased. Meanwhile, the Duke couldn't say nothing, of course, but he made all sorts of signs with his hands and made queer noises like *"Goo-goo-goo-goo"* all the time.

After supper, Mary Jane fetched the letter her father left behind and the King read it out loud and cried over it. It give the dwelling house and three thousand dollar in gold to the girls and all the property and houses and another three thousand to Harvey and William. It also told where that cash was hid down in the cellar. So then these two frauds said they'd go and fetch it up and have everything square and aboveboard, and told me to come along with a candle.

We shut the cellar door behind us and when they found the bag of gold they spilt it out on the floor and it was a lovely sight. My, the way the King's and the Duke's eyes did shine!

When we finally got upstairs, everybody gathered round the table and the King he counted it and stacked it up — twenty elegant little piles!

Everybody looked hungry at it, so they put it back in the bag again and the King says to the girls, "You take the money — take it all. We wouldn't dream of robbin' our dear nieces of a single cent." They was certainly playing the part of the loving uncles to the hilt, but I knew they was up to some skulduggery underneath it.

Before long a big iron-jawed man worked himself into the crowd from outside and stood silent, a-listening and a-looking. So the King goes on talking and he uses his words kind of too fancy and all wrong, putting on airs to seem like he thought the English speak. Well, so the iron-jawed man laughed right out in his face and everybody was shocked.

One of them says, "Why, Doctor Robinson, hain't you heard the news? This is Harvey Wilks."

The King smiled eager and tried to shake his hand.

"Keep your hands off me," says the doctor. "*You* talk like an Englishman — it's the worst imitation I ever heard! *You* Peter Wilks's brother! You're a fraud, that's what you are!"

By this time the poor girls was hanging onto the King and crying, when all of a sudden the doctor turns on them and says, "I warn you as a friend of your father's and yours too, to turn your backs on that scoundrel and have nothin' to do with him, the ignorant tramp! He's come here with a lot of empty names and facts which he picked up somewheres, and you take them for proofs. I beg you to turn this rascal out. Will you?"

Then Mary Jane straightened herself up and my, but she was handsome! "Here is my answer!" She hove up the bag of money and put it in the King's hands and says, "Take this six thousand dollars and invest it for us any way you want to, and we don't even ask a receipt."

Then she and the girls put their arms around the King, while everybody clapped their hands and stomped on the floor, and the King held up his head and smiled proud.

The Bag of Gold

WHEN at last everybody had left, the King asks Mary Jane where we was all to sleep and she told us we'd manage to fit in somehow, if the girls doubled up. The King and the Duke each had a room, plain but nice, and I had a little cubby up in the garret. I knowed now that I was among friends, and I begun to feel low-down and ornery 'cause I was sure as shooting them frauds was up to tricks again and would rob the girls of all that money unless someone stopped them. So I says to myself, I'll have that money for them or bust! I thought it all over and decided I'd best not tell anybody my suspicions yet, but I would steal the money and hide it, and by and by when I'm way down the river I'll write a letter and tell Mary Jane where it's hid. I'd better do what I got to do tonight 'cause the doctor might not let up talking. So, thinks I, first I'll go and search their rooms.

I went to the Duke's room and pawed around in the dark, but there warn't nothing there, then on into the King's room and was snooping around there when I hear 'em coming, so I thought I better hide me and eavesdrop. I slipped behind some of the clothes hanging on the wall and stood there perfectly still. I listened and learned how they was planning to skip out of there early in the morning 'cause they was afraid what that doctor might do. They was going to beat it with what they'd got right in their hands.

The Duke says, "I don't think we put that money in a good place," and that did interest me.

The King says, "Why?" and the Duke argues that someone will find it when they come to do the rooms tomorrow. So while I stuck there tight to the wall, the King comes a-fumbling under the curtain three foot from where I was and got the bag. He and the Duke took it and shoved it through a rip in the straw tick that was under the feather bed, and crammed it in amongst the straw, and said it was all safe now. Well, I knowed better. I had it out of there before they was halfway downstairs, and groped along up to my cubby and hid it there until I could get a chance to put it somewhere outside the house, 'cause if they missed it, every room would be ransacked. So I held on until all the late sounds had quit and then I slipped down the ladder with it.

I tiptoed downstairs all right and heard both the rascals snoring as I went by their rooms. I peeked through a crack of the dining room door and see the men that was watching the corpse all sound asleep on their chairs. The front door was locked and the key wasn't there, but just then I heard somebody coming down the stairs, so I run in the parlor. The only place I could see to hide the bag quick was right in the coffin. I tucked the money in under the lid, just down beyond where his hands was crossed and then I hid myself.

The person coming was Mary Jane. She went to the coffin and knelt down with her back to me. She didn't see me, so I managed to slip up to bed.

I was pretty uneasy now, thinking about what I'd done, 'cause the money would sure be found when they come to screw on the lid, and then the King would get it again. But it was too late to do anything more right then.

The funeral was the next day and the undertaker come with his man for the service. I see the coffin lid was the way it was before, but I dasn't go to look in under it with all the folks around. After the funeral sermon, which was good enough but long and tiresome, the undertaker begun to sneak up on the casket with his screwdriver. I was in a sweat then and watched him pretty keen,

but he never meddled at all, just slid the lid along, soft as mush, and screwed it down tight. So there I was! I didn't know if the money was still in there or not. How could I know what to write Mary Jane; she might dig him up and nothing would be there. I wished to goodness I'd just left the whole thing alone!

So they buried him and we come back home and I could see the King was in a lather to get away. But they was having an auction the next day to settle up that other property and the "uncles" had to stay. And the same day some slave-traders happened to come along and the King sold all the whole passel of slaves to him right off, but the poor girls was awful cut up about it, having not only to lose their good colored friends, but to see the Negro families all broke up besides.

That morning they missed the gold and the King and the Duke shook me awake and asked me if I was in their rooms last night. I said I warn't, but I did see a couple of the Negroes go in there once or twice.

"Great guns; this *is* a go," said the King, and both of 'em looked pretty sick and tolerable silly 'cause them Negroes was already sold and gone. I felt dreadful glad I'd worked it all off onto them and yet hadn't done the slaves no harm by it.

As I was going downstairs I passed the girls' room and seen Mary Jane in there. She'd been crying, so I asked what was the matter and she said she couldn't bear to think about those split-up slave families. So to comfort her I says, "But they will meet up again and inside of two weeks, I know it!"

Laws, it was out before I could think! So I says to myself, I'm a-goin' to chance it; I'll up and tell the whole truth this time. So I says to her, "Don't you holler, jest sit still and take it like a man. You want to brace up, Miss Mary, 'cause it's goin' to be hard for you, but it's the truth. These 'uncles' of yourn ain't no uncles at all. They're a couple of frauds, just like the Doc said, regular deadbeats."

It jolted her up like everything, but I went on and told her every blamed bit of it. She jumped up with her face afire like sunset and says:

"The brutes! Come, don't let's waste a minute, not a second! We'll have them tarred and feathered and flung into the river! You tell me what I'd ought to do and I'll do it."

I told her her uncles was a rough gang and that I had to travel with them awhile longer, but I'd rather not tell her why for the moment. If we was to blow on them, the town would get *me* out all right, but there'd be another person that she didn't know about that would be in big trouble (meaning Jim, of course). Now sudden I see how I could get both me and Jim outer this, get the frauds jailed here and leave, but I didn't want my plan to begin working till pretty late that night.

So I tells her to put a candle in her window a bit before eleven o'clock to show me that everything's all peaceful, and if I didn't turn up by then it would mean I'm gone, out of the way, and safe. Then she was to come right out and spread the news around and get these beats jailed. But if I didn't get away, and so got caught with them, then she'd got to stand by me and say I'd told her the whole thing beforehand.

"Stand by you, indeed, I will! They shan't touch a hair of your head!"

Then I says, "There's just one more thing — that bag o' money."

"Well, they've got that."

"No, they hain't."

"Why, who has it?"

"I wish I knowed. I had it 'cause I stole it from them to give to you and I know where I hid it, but I'm afraid it ain't there no more. I'm dreadful sorry, Miss Mary Jane, but I done the best I could."

She wanted to know, of course, where I'd hid it, but I says I'd ruther not tell her where, but I'd write it on a piece of paper, so I wrote, "I put it in the coffin. I was in there when you was cryin' there in the night. I was behind the door and I was mighty sorry for you, Miss Mary Jane."

I advised her to go that afternoon to visit a neighbor, just in case there was earlier trouble than we planned, so she said good-by to me and if she never saw me again she couldn't ever forget me and would pray for me too. Well, I hain't never seen her since she went out that door, but I reckon I've thought of her a million times.

That afternoon I was glad she warn't there, for there was the most awful to-do. When the steamboat landed, two strangers come up looking for the Wilkses, and claimed *they* was Harvey and William. Such a lot of arguing around, with the doctor and a lawyer there asking lots of questions and trying to get proofs!

Finally the new Uncle Harvey asks if there's anybody present who helped to lay out his brother for burying, 'cause he could tell 'em there was a tattoo mark on Peter's breast. He said he remembered it was three small letters — P.B.W. When the King heard this he turned white as a sheet, but he was game; he allowed as how the marks was not letters but just a small, thin blue arrow. Of course I knowed he made it up. But the two fellers who fixed up the body said they hadn't seen no such marks and so now everybody was in a state of mind, all yelling.

"The whole bilin' lot of 'em is frauds. Let's duck 'em all!"

But the lawyer ups and says, "Friends, there's one right way out. We'll go and dig up that corpse and have a look."

The crowd was for it, and shouted loud, "If we don't find either of them marks, we'll lynch the whole passel of 'em!"

This sure scared me as they gripped us all and marched us straight for the graveyard. It was only nine in the evening, but the sky was darkening up and lightning beginning to wink and flitter and the wind to shiver amongst the leaves. This was the most awful trouble and the most dangersome I ever was in. When we got out there, the crowd swarmed into the graveyard and they dug and dug like everything. It got even darker and the rain started and the wind swished and swushed along and the lightning come brisker and brisker.

At last they had out the coffin and begun to unscrew the lid. And then such a crowding and shoving you never did see. All of a sudden the lightning let go a perfect sluice of white glare and somebody sings out, "By the living jingo, here's the bag of gold on his breast!"

With all the excitement then, I saw a way to skin out of there, so I lit for the road in the dark and made tracks.

When I struck the town, I see there warn't nobody out in the storm and just as I was sailing by the Wilks's house, *flash* comes the light in Mary Jane's window! My heart swelled out sudden, like to bust. She was the best girl I ever hope to meet. I ran on to the river's edge and borrowed the first boat I come to and put out for the towhead. I was so fagged when I struck the raft I could only gasp, "Out with you, Jim, and set her loose! We're shut of them!"

So in two seconds, away we went a-sliding down the river again. But before we could be too joyous about being free once more, I heard a sound I knowed mighty well. It was the King and the Duke just a-laying to their oars and making their skiff hum!

So I wilted right down onto the planks and give up. It was all I could do to keep from crying.

The minute they got aboard, of course, a big argument started, and the King went for me and shook me.

"Tryin' to give us the slip, was ye? You pup! Tired of our company, hey?"

I said, "Oh, no, your Majesty, we warn't."

"What was your idea, then?"

"'Twarn't no idea, but it happened this way. When they was draggin' us all down to the graveyard to see them marks on the corpse, everybody got so excited when they seen the gold they let go their holt on us, and that's when I made a run for it, and I reckon that's what saved your hides too."

They was still a minute — thinking — and then the King says, "We reckoned the Negroes stole it."

So the King and the Duke started at each other hot and heavy, as to who put that gold in the coffin. Neither of 'em knew; each accused the other. I said nothing. Finally, for the sake of quiet, the King confessed he had the idea and owned up, although it warn't true. This seemed to satisfy the Duke, so the King sneaked into the wigwam and took to his bottle for comfort and before long the Duke tackled his, and in about half an hour they was thick as thieves again. When they got to snoring, Jim and I had a long gabble, and I told him everything.

We dasn't stop at any town for days and days. We was down south in the warm weather now and a mighty long ways from home, so the frauds reckoned they was out of danger and they begun to work the villages again. They tried most of their old tricks, but all of it come to nothing; they got just about dead broke. They was dreadful blue and desperate, but began to lay their heads together in the wigwam, talking low and confidential for hours at a time. Jim and me got uneasy 'cause we judged they was studying up some kind of worse deviltry, so we decided we ought to shake 'em for good soon as ever we could.

Old Friends

WELL, EARLY one morning we all hid the raft near a shabby little village named Pikesville and the King went ashore to smell around to see if anyone had got wind of the "Royal Nonesuch." So the rest of us stayed behind and waited, but he was off a powerful long time, and we thought someone better go after him.

When the Duke and I got to the village, we found the King in a little low doggery, very drunk. The Duke began to abuse him right away and they started to fight. I said to myself that this was my chance and lit out for the raft, but when I got there and called Jim, there warn't no answer. He was gone! I shouted and called him over and over, but it warn't no use. I just set down and cried then, I couldn't help it.

But I didn't set still long and soon wandered out along the road where I run across a boy and asked him if he'd seen a strange Negro and he said, yes, he had. He said he was down at Silas Phelps's place, for they caught him. "He's a runaway slave, you know, and there's two hundred dollars reward on him."

I says, "Who nailed him?"

"It was an old feller, a stranger, and he sold out his share in him for forty dollars 'cause he said he had to go up river and couldn't wait."

That sounded powerful suspicious to me. That was sure enough the King. But how could he turn that way against good old Jim, and send him back to slavery for just forty dirty dollars?

I went back then to the raft and sat down in the wigwam to think. I was full of trouble and didn't know what to do next. But at last it all come clear; I would go to work and steal Jim out of slavery again! So I set right back for shore, and the first person I met was the Duke. He was sticking up bills again for the "Royal Nonesuch." He seemed awful surprised and displeased to see me. I reckon he was pretty scared by this time that somebody was going to blow on him and that other fraud.

So I says then, "You see Jim anywheres?"

"No, that old fool has gone and sold him and never divided the price with me, so *that* money's gone."

It was plain that Duke wanted to get shut of me, so I left him quick, then doubled back, where he couldn't see me, toward the Phelps's place where that boy had said Jim was. I wanted to get to him and stop his mouth until the King and the Duke got away. It would be bad if he talked and got us all back into trouble.

Phelps's was one of these little one-horse cotton plantations — a rail fence around a two-acre yard, big double log-house for the white folks, smoke-house, little log cabins for the Negroes on t'other side, and one small hut all by itself, and lots of hounds asleep all roundabout.

I went around and clumb over the back fence and started for the kitchen, but the hounds woke right up and went for me. A slave-woman come out the door and bid them be quiet, and at the same time a middle-aged white woman come running from the house, and behind her comes her little children. She was just smiling all over and calls out, "It's you at last, ain't it?"

I out with a "Yes'm" before I thought.

So she says to the children, "It's your cousin Tom. Tell him howdy!"

They still hid behind her and she run on, "We been expecting you for a couple of days or more. What kep' you? Boat run aground?"

"Yes'm" says I, "she —"

"Don't you say 'Yes'm.' Say Aunt Sally. Your uncle's been uptown every day to fetch you and he's just gone again. Didn't you meet him?"

"No, I didn't seen nobody, Aunt Sally." I thought that was safe.

Right then an old gentleman walks in and says, "Why, who's this?"

"It's Tom Sawyer, Silas, at last."

By jings, I most slumped through the floor. They was all so joyful to see me, but it warn't nothing to my feelings, for it was like being born again. It was real helpful to find out who I was!

So they got asking me all kinds of questions while they was making me welcome and I told them more about the Sawyers than ever happened to any six Sawyer families, talking until my chin was so tired it couldn't hardly go any more.

Suddenly, off in the distance I heard a steamboat whistle and I got to thinking all at once what would happen if Tom was on that boat and how I ought to waylay him and throw him a wink to keep quiet. So I made an excuse about fetching my baggage, and they let me take their wagon and I started uptown. Sure enough, there in another wagon, coming right along, was Tom Sawyer himself, just as I'd thought. He looked at me as if he'd seen a ghost and said, "What you want to come back and ha'nt me for, Huck Finn?"

I says, "I hain't come back, 'cause I hain't never been gone."

"Don't you play nothin' on me," Tom went on. "Honest Injun, you ain't a ghost?"

I told him I certainly warn't. "I never was murdered. I played it on them. You come across here and feel me, if you don't believe it."

So he done that and it satisfied him and he was glad. He wanted to know all about everything I'd been doing, 'cause it was a grand adventure and mysterious, just what he liked best.

Then I says, "Tom, there's something I ought to tell you first off, and that is there's a Negro here that I'm trying to steal out of slavery, and it's old Miss Watson's Jim!"

And Tom says, "What! Jim?"

So I says, "I know it's a dirty low-down business, but I'm a-goin' through with it, and I want you to keep mum and not let on. Will you?"

His eye lit up and he says, "Why, I'll even help you steal him."

At first I thought he must be joking. I couldn't believe it. Tom Sawyer a slave-stealer!

Right then we made a plan. Tom told me to go on back ahead of him, take along his trunk and pretend it was mine. Then he would turn up a little later and I was not to let on I knew him. So I done just what he said; I always do. And when Tom's wagon finally drove up, Aunt Sally see it through the window and says, "Why, here's somebody else coming. Wonder who it is."

The whole family went right out to meet him and Tom let himself be persuaded to come in and he told them he come from Hicksville, Ohio, and his name was William Thompson, and he made a bow. He sat down and run on and on, making up stuff about Hicksville, and then suddenly he reached over and kissed Aunt Sally right on the mouth.

"You owdacious puppy," she scolded. "I'm surprised at you."

"But they — they — told me you would like it!"

"They told you? Who's they?"

Then Tom looks around at me and says, "Don't you think Aunt Sally'd open out her arms and say 'Sid Sawyer —' "

"My land!" she exclaims. "You impudent young rascal, to fool a body so! We warn't looking for *you* at all, but only Tom. Sis never wrote to me about anybody coming but him."

That night we had the best dinner yet, because there was things on that table enough for seven families — and all hot, too — none of your flabby tough meat that's laid in a damp cellar cupboard all night.

After the meal, one of the children asks Uncle Silas if him and Tom and me couldn't go to the show in town. The old man said no, 'cause he reckoned there warn't going to be any, on account of the runaway slave had told all about that business of the two frauds and the scandalous goings on. He figured that by now they'd been run out of town.

So Tom and me decided we better hurry and warn them fellers, because any trouble they'd get into might pretty well include me. So we said we was tired and would go right up to bed, but instead we slid out the window of our room, down the lightning rod and shoved for the town.

On our way along I told Tom the whole story about our "Royal Nonesuch" rapscallions, and as we neared the place here comes a raging rush of people with torches and an awful whooping and yelling and banging tin pans, and I see they had the pore King and the Duke astraddle of a rail. They was all over tar and feathers and looked like a couple of monstrous big soldier plumes. Well, it made me sick to see it and I was sorry for them pitiful rascals. Human beings can be awful cruel to one another and I couldn't ever feel any hardness against them no more. But we see we was too late — we couldn't do no good, so we poked along back home.

Prisoner's Plot

TOM SAYS to me next morning, "I bet I know where Jim is hid. He's down in that hut by the fence. I see a slave-boy yesterday going in there with a watermelon, and you can't think that was to feed the hounds, can you? I seen the boy open the padlock when he went in, and shut it tight again when he came out. He fetched uncle a key about the time we got up from table — the same key, I bet. Now Huck, work your mind and help me figure out a plan for stealin' Jim away."

So I says, "First off we got to find out if it *is* Jim, and then just steal the key out of the old man's breeches after he's in bed, let Jim out and all beat it for the raft and the river."

But Tom said that plan wouldn't work, 'cause it was too blamed simple. So he come up with one that was awful complicated, but worth fifteen of mine for style. It would be real mysterious, troublesome, and good. We went right out and looked over the hut and Tom says, "We're going to dig him out, of course! We'll go through the lean-to, and break our way into it."

So then we went back to make friends with the Negro who took out food every day to the hut, and we persuaded him to let us go in there with him. Sure enough, it was Jim! He grabs us by the hands and squeezes them, and we whispers to him, "Don't ever let on to know us, and if you hear any digging going on nights, it's friends. We're going to set you free."

The next few days we was mighty busy figuring out all the pieces of Tom's plan. He wanted everything to be exactly like all them prisoners' adventures in the books he reads. He said we had to have what I thought was all kinds of blamed foolish things such as an old rusty saw, to cut off the leg of Jim's bed he was chained to (it would be too simple just to lift up the bed and slip the chain off); a rope ladder made of torn sheets, for him to escape on (although he was on the ground floor already); an old shirt for him to write his diary on in blood; pens to write with made from old candlesticks or pewter spoons; tin plates for him to toss out with messages scratched on them, and a lot of other stuff. Tom said that everything was all right now except for tools.

"Tools for what?" I asks.

"Why, to dig with. We ain't a-goin' to gnaw him out, are we?"

"Well, what about all them shovels and picks that's standin' around in there?"

"Why, Huck Finn, did you ever hear of a prisoner having all the modern conveniences right to his hand to dig with?"

"Well, what *do* we need, then?"

"A couple of case knives to dig a hole through the foundations. We can't risk takin' much time, though, 'cause Uncle Silas is sure to hear soon where Jim come from. He's already writ to New Orleans, he said."

That very night, after folks had gone to bed, we went down to the lean-to and got to work, and we dug and dug with the case knives till 'most midnight, and all we got was blisters. I told Tom this warn't no way to hurry. Tom agreed with me. We'd have to dig him out with the picks and let on that they was case knives. So we did and soon had a hole big enough to get through, and we decided that now the time had come to take the things in to Jim. So we slips through easy and gives the stuff to him, some each night.

Jim told us we warn't his only visitors, that Uncle Silas and Aunt Sally come in every day or so to see if he was comfortable and well fed, and to pray with him. This time we told him the biggest secret, that we was going to bake a rope ladder in a pie for him and send it in by the Negro boy; and he'd better look when he could in Uncle Silas' coat pockets and Aunt Sally's apron when they come, 'cause there might be some other things smuggled in there for him. Jim had plenty of corncob pipes and tobacco, so we had right good sociable times most every night. Once we even let him all the way out to help us drag in a heavy grindstone we needed, and it seemed kind of silly to shut him up again, but Tom said we had to.

We had a lot of trouble baking that pie for the rope ladder. We warn't no cooks and didn't have no kitchen to work in, but we finally got it done pretty good, and sent it in to him with the tin plates hid in the bottom.

That old grindstone he helped us drag in was for him to scratch mournful inscriptions on, and Tom took one of the pens we'd filed out of the brass candlestick and wrote out the following — "HERE A CAPTIVE HEART BUSTED," which I thought was real sad.

So far, so good, but Tom went on having new ideas. He said that all prisoners had to have pets of some kind — snakes or spiders or rats. Jim objected to snakes and spiders, but we told him he'd have to have something to tame, so we just picked the rats for him. Jim didn't like that much better, so Tom settled for something else. He says, "I know what — we'll get a flower for you to water with your tears!"

Jim said it was too dark in there to raise anything but a mullen stalk, and he warn't going to cry enough tears to water that, which made Tom kind of mad.

Well, by the end of three weeks things was in pretty good shape. Jim had everything Tom had dreamed up, and the bed leg was sawed off, and we'd even et the sawdust. Now Tom said it was time for the "nonnamous letters."

"What's them?" I asks.

"Warnings to folks that something's up. If we don't give them notice, there won't be nobody nor nothing to interfere with us, and so after all our hard work and trouble this escape will go off perfectly flat."

I says, "That's just the way I'd like it," but Tom looked disgusted with me.

So he begins to write, and the first letter said, *"Beware! Trouble is brewing. Keep a sharp lookout."* It was signed *Unknown Friend*.

So I took it and shoved it under the front door late that night, like Tom told me to. Next night we stuck a picture which Tom drawed in his blood, of a skull and crossbones on the front door, and the third night another one, of a coffin on the back door. My, but that family was in a sweat when they see them, and was Tom tickled! The whole thing was working very well; he said it showed it was done right. So now for the grand bulge!

We heard them say at supper they was going to have one of the Negroes on watch at each door all night, so Tom said it was time to send the last letter. It said:

There is a desprate gang of cutthroats from over in the Indian Territory going to steal your runaway slave tonight. I am one of the gang, but I've got religgion and wish to quit, and so will betray the hellish design. They will sneak down along the fence at midnight exact with a false key and go into the cabin to get him. I will Bah like a sheep as soon as they get in and whilst they're getting the chains loose, you slip over and lock them in, so you can kill them at your leasure. I do not ask any reward but just to know I've done right.

Unknown Friend.

So we made sure the raft and the canoe was ready for the escape, and when the big night come, Tom went to the cabin to stay by Jim and I had to sneak down cellar to collect some provisions for the trip. Whilst I was creeping upstairs with some butter, I seen a big crowd there in the setting room, about fifteen farmers, and every one of 'em had a gun, all fidgeting and uneasy.

As I stood there listening I heard one of them say, "I'm for going to the cabin first and catching them when they come!"

Aunt Sally seen me then and said, "Now you clear right out of here and go up to bed. Don't lemme see no more of you tonight!"

BEWARE!
TROUBLE IS BREWING
KEEP A SHARP LOOKOUT
unknown friend

I was upstairs in a second and down the lightning rod in another one, and shinning through the dark to the lean-to. I told Tom we must jump for it now, and not a minute to lose — the house was full of armed men.

Tom's eyes shone with pleasure. "No! You don't say! Ain't that bully!"

But he didn't lose no time. It was so dark I couldn't see Jim, but Tom had got him all ready and it was now time to slide out and give the sheep signal. Then we heard the tramp of the men at the door and one of them begins to fumble with the padlock.

Somebody said, "The door's locked, they haven't come yet, so some of you stay here and lay for them in the dark and kill 'em."

When they broke in, they couldn't see us in the dark and most trod on us while we was hustling to slide under the bed, but we made it all right and on out through the hole, swift and soft, through the lean-to toward the fence. Jim and me got over it all right, but Tom's britches caught on a splinter in the top rail and then he had to pull loose sudden which made a noise, and as he started off after us somebody sings out, "Who goes there? Answer or I'll shoot."

But we didn't stop to answer; we just unfurled our heels and shoved. Then there was a rush and a *Bang-Bang-Bang!* and the bullets fairly whizzed around us! We heard them sing out, "Here they are! They've broke for the river! After 'em, boys, and turn loose the dogs!"

Then they come right along, full tilt. We struck up through the bush to where the canoe was tied, hopped in and pulled for dear life towards the middle of the river.

When we got to the island where the raft was I says, *"Now,* old Jim, you're a free man, and I bet you won't ever be a slave no more!"

"En a mighty good job it wuz, too, Huck. It 'uz planned beautiful, en it 'uz *done* beautiful; en dey ain't *nobody* kin git up a plan dat's mo' mixed up en splendid den what dat one wuz."

We was all as glad as we could be, but Tom was the gladdest of all because he had a bullet in the calf of his leg. But it warn't no light wound and was bleeding considerable. We bandaged it the best we could, but soon Jim and I seen there was a doctor needed.

Tom raised big objections to this, but when he sees me getting the canoe ready he says, "Well, then, if you're bound to go, I'll tell you what to do when you get to the village. Shut the door and blindfold the doctor tight and fast, swear him to silence, and put a purse full of gold in his hand and then lead him in a roundabout way amongst the islands till you get back here."

So just to keep him quiet I said I'd do all that, and left, but warned Jim to be sure to go hide in the woods when he see the doctor coming.

Happy Ending

I FOUND a doctor, a nice, kind old fellow, and told him I had a friend who had just shot himself in a dream by accident. He laughed at that, but come along with me just the same. I got to thinking, if it's a long job and he can't fix Tom's leg right away, we'll just have to hold him prisoner on the raft. So I took him to the canoe to paddle over by himself, 'cause I was bilin' with curiosity to know what went on now at the Phelpses and just had to go and snoop there.

Along the path in the dark I run smack into Uncle Silas, who said, "Why, Tom, where you been all this time, you rascal? Your aunt's been mighty uneasy."

"I hain't been nowheres," I says. "Only just huntin' for the runaway slave — me and Sid."

"Where's Sid now?"

"Around town somewhere, smelling out news."

So I went along home with him and when we got there Aunt Sally was that glad to see me she laughed and cried both, and give me a little licking, too, that was only affection. She wanted to know right away where Sid was, and I see my chance and told her I'd run up to town and get him.

"No, you won't," she says. "One is enough to be lost at a time. If he's not here for supper, your uncle will go."

He warn't there for supper and of course Uncle Silas didn't find him neither, but I couldn't manage to get away that night without hurting their feelings, although goodness knows I wanted to see how Tom was.

The old man was up at dawn, but couldn't get no track of Tom and pretty soon said to Aunt Sally, "Say, did I ever give you that letter?"

"What letter?"

"The one I got at the post office yesterday."

She says, "No, you didn't!" So he went off to fetch it from somewheres he'd laid it down, and handed it to her. She give it a look and says, "Why, it's from Sis in St. Petersburg!"

Before she could even break it open, she dropped it and run, for she see something through the window, and so did I. It was Tom Sawyer on a stretcher, and that old doctor, and Jim there, too, with his hands tied behind him, and a lot of people with them.

Aunt Sally flung herself right at Tom, crying, "Oh, he's dead! He's dead! I knowed it."

And Tom turned his head and muttered something or other that showed he warn't in his right mind, so she threw up her hands and shouted, "He's alive, thank God, and that's enough!"

The crowd begun muttering now that they ought to hang Jim right off, but the doctor, he pleaded for him and said how he had been such a help caring for the wounded boy and hadn't give a thought to his own safety, and that he wasn't a bad fellow at all. Then he told how some men had come along by the raft in a skiff and had taken Jim prisoner right before his eyes and that he hadn't done nothing to deserve it.

So everyone begun to soften and promised they wouldn't be too hard on Jim, so they locked him up for a while and wasn't going to hang him yet.

I was worrying real hard, not only about Jim, but about whether I'd better tell Aunt Sally how Tom happened to get shot, but I put this off and thank goodness he was better in the morning and she clean forgot to ask. But Tom wakes up in his right mind and stared at us and says, "Well, hello . . . I'm at home! What happened to Jim and the raft and all?"

So then there was no help for it — the whole story had to come out. We told Aunt Sally how Tom and me set Jim free and done the whole planning all ourselves, and she says as how she'd never heard the likes of it in all her born days. She called us rapscallions, but I see she was really proud of us. Then she warned us not to meddle with Jim no more.

Tom looks at me very grave then and says, "Look here, now, didn't you tell me he was all right? Hasn't Jim got away after all?"

" 'Deed he hasn't," says Aunt Sally. "They got him locked up in that cabin again, loaded down with chains till he's claimed or hanged."

Tom rose square up in bed at that, with his eyes blazing, and sings out to me, "They hain't got no *right* to shut him up. Shove now! Turn him loose! He ain't no slave — he's as free as any cretur that walks this earth!"

"Whatever does the child mean?"

"I mean every word I say, Aunt Sally. If you don't go free him now, I swear I'll do it. I've knowed him all my life and so has Tom, there. His owner, old Miss Watson, died two months ago and she was ashamed she was ever goin' to sell him down the river, and said so, and set him free in her will."

"Then what on earth did *you* want to set him free again for?"

"Well, that *is* a question, I must say, and *just* like women! Why, we wanted the adventure of it — and I would have waded neck-deep in blood to — goodness alive, why, AUNT POLLY!"

Well, if she warn't sure enough standing there, just inside the door, looking as sweet as an angel half full of pie, I wish I may never!

Aunt Sally jumped for her and most hugged the head off her and cried over her. But I found a good enough place for me under the bed, for it was getting pretty sultry for us. As I peeked out, Aunt Polly begun looking across at Tom over her spectacles, kind of grinding him into the earth.

"Yes," she said, "I'd sure turn my head away if I was you, Tom!"

"Oh, deary me," says Aunt Sally, "is he changed so? It ain't Tom. It's Sid. Now, where is that Tom? He was just here a minute ago."

"You mean where's Huck Finn. I reckon I hain't raised such a scamp as my Tom all these years not to know him when I see him. Come out from under that bed, Huck Finn. Tom was right, though, about old Miss Watson. Didn't you get any of my letters? I wrote you twice to ask what you meant in yours about Sid being here."

"Well, I never got 'em, Sis."

So Aunt Polly, she turns round slow and severe and says, "You, Tom, you hand out those letters!"

He squirms a little and says, "I hid 'em, but they're just like they was when I got 'em out of the office. It would have spoiled our whole plot if Aunt Sally had read 'em."

"What about the last one I wrote to say I was coming down to see you all?"

"No," says Aunt Sally, "Tom didn't take that one. It come yesterday. I hain't read it yet, but it's all right, I've got it right here safe."

Well, we had Jim out of his chains in no time and they even let him come up in the sick room and nurse Tom, who gave Jim some dollars he had for being prisoner for us so patient, and doing it up so good. Jim was most pleased to death because now he was truly free.

Then Tom says right away, "As soon as we can, let's all three of us slide out of here one of these nights and get an outfit and go for some howling adventure, maybe over in Indian Territory. What do you say?"

"Well," I says, "I can't do it exactly. I ain't got no money for an outfit, and if I get to earn any, my Pap is goin' to catch up with me one of these days and snatch it way from me, like he always does."

Jim says then kind of solemn, "He ain't ever a-goin' to catch up with you, Huck. Doan' you remember de house dat 'uz float'n down de river and dey 'uz a man in dah, kivered up, en I went in en looked at him? Well, now you kin do anythin' you pleases, cuz dat man wuz your Pap!"

There's nothing much more to tell here. Tom's most well now and wears his bullet on a watch guard around his neck, but I reckon I got to light out for the Territory ahead of the rest because Aunt Sally, she's going to adopt me and sivilize me and I can't stand that. I been there before!